# Princess Smartypants

### Babette Cole

PUFFIN

Princess Smartypants did not want
to get married. She enjoyed being a Ms.

Because she was very pretty and rich,
all the princes wanted her to be their Mrs.

Princess Smartypants wanted to live in her castle
with her pets and do exactly as she pleased.

"It's high time you smartened yourself up," said her mother, the Queen. "Stop messing about with those animals and find yourself a husband!"

Suitors were always turning up at the castle
making a nuisance of themselves.
"Right," declared Princess Smartypants,
"whoever can accomplish the tasks
that I set will, as they say,
win my hand."

She asked Prince Compost to
stop the slugs eating
her garden.

She asked
Prince Rushforth
to feed her pets.

She challenged
Prince Pelvis to a
roller-disco marathon.

She invited Prince Boneshaker
for a cross-country ride
on her motorbike.

She called on Prince Vertigo
to rescue her from her tower.

She sent Prince Bashthumb to chop some firewood in the royal forest.

She suggested to Prince Fetlock
that he might like to put her
pony through its paces.

She told Prince Grovel to take
her mother, the Queen, shopping.

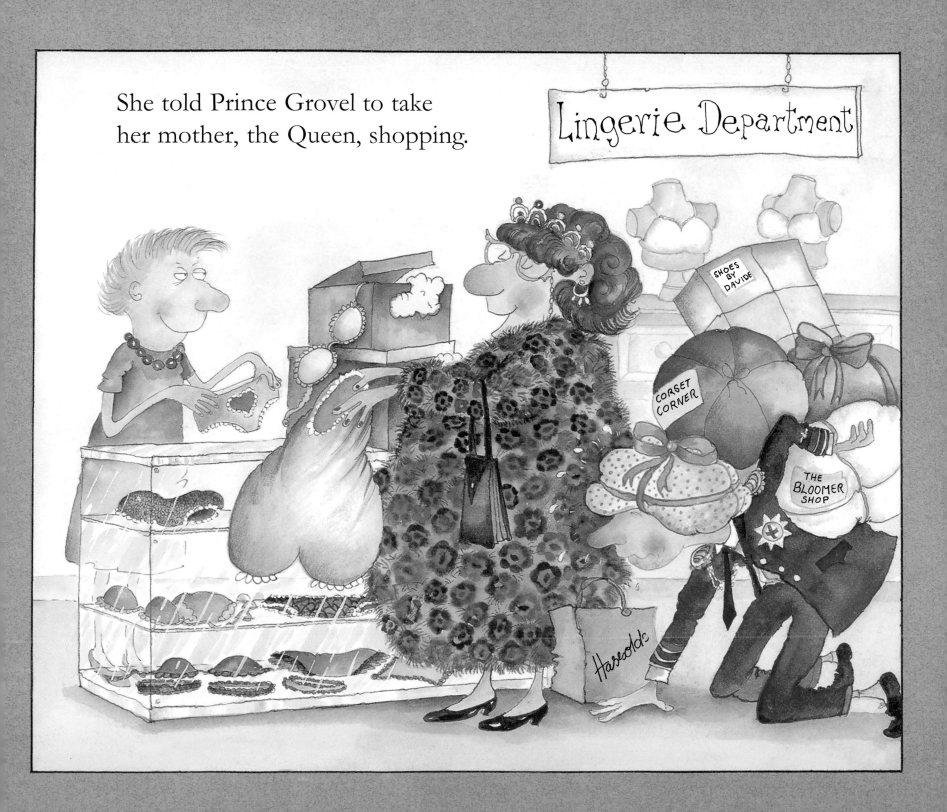

She commanded Prince Swimbladder
to retrieve her magic ring
from the goldfish pond.

None of the princes could accomplish
the task he was set. They all left in disgrace.
"That's that then," said Smartypants,
thinking she was safe.

Then Prince Swashbuckle
turned up.

He stopped the slugs eating her garden...

...fed her pets...

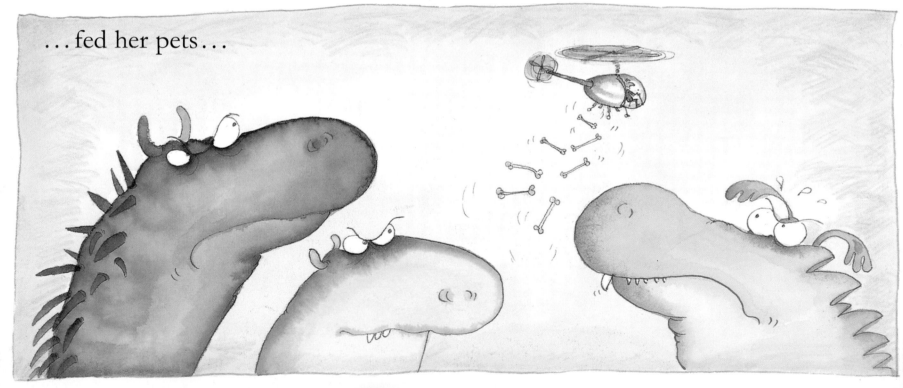

...roller-discoed
until dawn...

...rode for miles
on her motorbike...

He rescued her
from her tower.

He found some firewood to chop in the forest.

He even tamed her horrid pony...

...took her mother, the Queen, shopping

and retrieved her magic ring from the goldfish pond.

Prince Swashbuckle didn't think Princess Smartypants was so smart.

So she gave him a magic kiss...

...and he turned
into a gigantic
warty toad!

Prince Swashbuckle left in a big hurry!

When the other princes heard what had happened to Prince Swashbuckle, none of them wanted to marry Smartypants…

…so she lived happily ever after.